ROTTEN RALPH'S
TRICK OR TREAT!

Written by Jack Gantos and Illustrated by Nicole Rubel

Houghton Mifflin Company

Boston

For Astro and Roger

—J.G.

For my family

—N.R.

Library of Congress Cataloging-in-Publication Data

Gantos, Jack.
  Rotten Ralph's trick or treat!

  Summary: Sarah's rotten cat Ralph goes to a
Halloween costume party dressed as her and creates
horrible mischief under the protection of his disguise.
  [1. Cats—Fiction. 2. Halloween—Fiction. 3. Costume
—Fiction. 4. Parties—Fiction.] I. Rubel, Nicole, ill.
II. Title.
PZ7.G15334Rom   1986   [E]   86-7276
ISBN 0-395-38943-7

The character of Rotten Ralph was originally created
by Nicole Rubel and Jack Gantos.

Printed in the United States of America

RNF ISBN 0-395-38943-7
PAP ISBN 0-395-48655-6

WOZ 10 9 8 7

Rotten Ralph is Sarah's rotten cat.

One day when Sarah came home early from school, Rotten Ralph was wearing a frightening Halloween mask.

Ralph and Sarah went inside.

Suddenly, a creepy hand slipped a note under the door.

"Look," said Sarah. "We've been invited to a costume party.

"It reads, COME AS THE THING YOU LOVE BEST. And because we are best friends," she said, "we'll go as each other."

That night Rotten Ralph and Sarah put on their costumes.

"Oh, Ralph," said Sarah. "No one will guess we're dressed as each other."

But Rotten Ralph didn't like his costume.

"I'd rather go as myself," he thought.

Just then the doorbell rang.

"Trick or treat!" shouted some children.

Rotten Ralph tricked them. He tossed all of his old cat food into their bags.

"That's not very nice," said Sarah.

On their way to the party, Rotten Ralph felt rotten. He chased a black cat right across Sarah's path.

"Oh no!" she cried. "That's bad luck! I hope this doesn't ruin the party."

When Ralph and Sarah arrived at the party,
everyone was fooled by their costumes.

"You look nice," they said to Ralph.

"Thank you," said Sarah.

"And you look nice, too," they said to Sarah.

But Rotten Ralph didn't want to be nice. As
soon as he spotted their Halloween candy, he
put it all in his bag.

After that, he pulled the sheets off the ghosts.

"That's no way for a best friend to act," said Sarah.

Then he poured the goldfish
into the punch bowl.

Everyone at the party was upset.

"What's wrong with Sarah?" one of them asked.

"She's never acted like this before,"
remarked another.

"I don't know what's gotten into her," said
the party hostess. "But I wish she'd behave
like that nice cat of hers."

Rotten Ralph ran into the kitchen.

He took the lid off the popcorn popper.

Popcorn flew all over the room.

Then he decorated the bathroom with candy apples.

"Stop it," said Sarah. "Everyone thinks I'm the rotten one."

The party guests had had enough of Sarah's rotten behavior.

"We think you should take your cat and go home," the hostess said to Ralph.

The real Sarah was embarrassed.

Rotten Ralph was happy to leave.

But Sarah was upset.

"A best friend wouldn't treat me this way," she sobbed.

Just then that black cat appeared.

"Oh NO!" cried Sarah. "Not more bad luck."

Rotten Ralph took off his costume.

"GROWLLL!" he howled. He chased the black cat out of Sarah's path and up a tree.

When they got home Sarah said,

"Oh, Ralph, you're still my best friend."

Rotten Ralph purred.

"Trick or treat!" he thought.

Then he curled up on Sarah's lap.